Max
Goes Fishing

Grosset & Dunlap
An Imprint of Penguin Group (USA) Inc.

Based upon the animated series *Max & Ruby*
A Nelvana Limited production © 2002–2003.

Max & Ruby © Rosemary Wells. Licensed by Nelvana Limited. NELVANA is a registered trademark of Nelvana Limited. CORUS is a trademark of Corus Entertainment Inc. All rights reserved. Published in 2013 by Grosset & Dunlap, a division of Penguin Young Readers Group, 345 Hudson Street, New York, New York 10014. GROSSET & DUNLAP is a trademark of Penguin Group (USA) Inc. Manufactured in China.

ISBN 978-0-448-46482-4   10 9 8 7 6 5 4 3 2

ALWAYS LEARNING   PEARSON

Ruby and her Bunny Scout friends were going to the lake to get their canoeing badges.

Max wanted to use his new fishing rod with his rubber duckie.

"Big fish!" said Max.

"I bet you'll catch a big fish, Max," said Ruby. "Make sure you stay right here on the dock, while we paddle our canoe!"

The scouts could hardly wait for their turns in the canoe.
One of the Bunny Scout leaders said, "First, paddle out
and back across the lake.

Then pull the canoe in and dock it by putting the rope over the post. When you're done, you will each get your badge." Just then, Ruby heard someone call her name.

It was Max. He was having trouble. His fishing line had a great big knot! Ruby untangled it.

"Catching a big fish!" said Max.

"That's right!" said Ruby.

Ruby returned to the Bunny Scouts and watched
Valerie speed across the lake.
But someone called Ruby's name again.

It was Max. He was twisted up in his fishing line. Ruby helped untangle him.

Now it was Louise's turn to paddle across the lake.
Ruby heard her name called again.

"Big fish!" said Max.
But Max had only caught a rubber boot on his line.

Now it was Ruby's turn to paddle. She started off across the lake. Everyone cheered.

Ruby turned the canoe perfectly and started to paddle back to the dock.

When she pulled in, she threw the rope over the docking
post just like the Bunny Scout leader had told her.
But she didn't notice Max's fishing line.

"Great job, Bunny Scouts! It's time for us to get our badges and sew them on!" said the Bunny Scout leader.

Everyone was very excited—even Max.

Suddenly the canoe came undocked.
"Look!" said Ruby. "Our canoe is floating away!"

"What will we do?" asked the rest of the Bunny Scouts.
"It's too deep to wade out!"

Max had an idea. He threw his line out to the canoe
and pulled it in.

"Hooray!" cheered the scouts.

They all got their badges.

"And you get a special rescue badge, Max!" said the Bunny Scout leader.